LASTING IMPRESSIONS

Story Concept: Suzanne Harper
Story Manuscript: Alessandro Ferrari
Art: GG Studio
Executive Chief: Giuliano Monni
Pencils: Vincenzo Cucca
Paint: Barbara Ciardo
Paint support: Andrea Errico, Alessia Nocera, Angelo Amorelli
Art Optimization: Stefano Attardi, Kawaii Creative Studio

CHAPTER 2
Layout: Giuseppe Manunta

CHAPTER 4
Layout: Giuseppe Manunta, Clean-up: Elena Pianta, Paint and Art Optimization: Kawaii Creative Studio,
Art Optimization: Stefano Attardi, Marco Ghiglione

CHAPTER 6
Layout: Giuseppe Manunta, Clean up: Elena Pianta
Colors: Kawaii Creative Studio, Art Optimization: Stefano Attardi, Kawaii Creative Studio

Based on the Disney Channel Original Movie
"High School Musical," Written by Peter Barsocchini
Based on the Disney Channel Original Movie
"High School Musical 2," Written by Peter Barsocchini
Based on Characters Created by Peter Barsocchini

DISNEP PRESS

NEW YORK

6128 - 142 Ave.

T5A - U5

Printed in the United States of America

Library of Congress Catalog Card Number on file.

ISBN 978-1-4231-1190-0

1 3 5 7 9 10 6 8 4 2

CHAPTER ONE

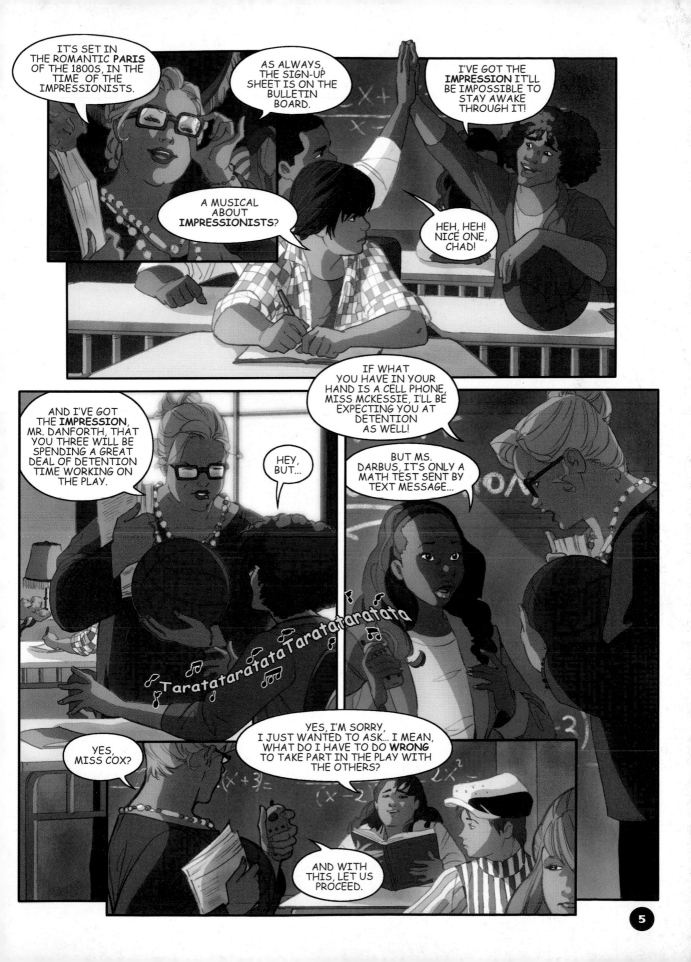

7

CHAPTER TWO

MESSAGE FROM GABRIELLA: "GOOD MORNING, SLEEPYHEAD! ;) YOU CAN'T IMAGINE THE DREAM I HAD LAST NIGHT..."

"REMEMBER THE PLACE WHERE WE FIRST MET, IN THE MOUNTAINS?"

"BUT THIS TIME IT WAS DIFFERENT. TAYLOR, CHAD AND THE OTHERS WERE THERE, TOO. EVEN MS. DARBUS..."

"...IT WAS LIKE BEING AT SCHOOL..."

"THEN I LOOKED AT MYSELF AND SUDDENLY... I WAS IN PAJAMAS!"

"THEN YOU SHOWED UP. YOU WERE IN PAJAMAS, TOO!"

"EVERYONE WAS IN PAJAMAS, AND WE WERE ALL SINGING AND DANCING. THE WHOLE WORLD WAS SINGING AND DANCING IN PAJAMAS!"

19

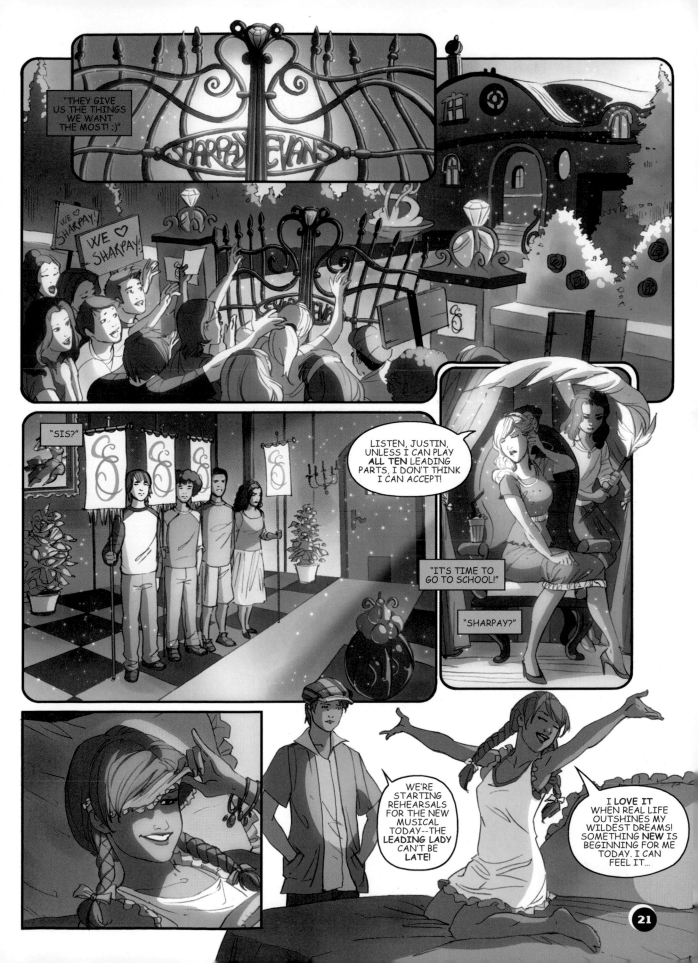

23

WE AREN'T GOING TO YOUR STUPID GAME, BUT... TOMORROW, REHEARSALS ARE SUSPENDED... UNTIL THE DAY AFTER TOMORROW!

AND NO, IT DOESN'T MEAN I'LL GO OUT WITH YOU, ZEKE, EVEN IF YOU MANAGE TO GIVE ME THE LIGHTING I DESERVE!

NOW, LET'S GET TO WORK!

SHE CALLED ME BY MY NAME... SHARPAY KNOWS MY NAME!

"YOU WERE GREAT TODAY..."

JEAN-LUC NEEDS TO BE MORE SURPRISED TO SEE HER. HE SINGS AS IF SHE WERE A GHOST, A DREAM...

ZEKE, THE LIGHTING NEEDS TO BE SOFTER...

WE NEED TO LEAVE AS MUCH SPACE AS POSSIBLE BETWEEN THE PROPS. AND RYAN, WE NEED THE CHOREOGRAPHY TO BE SLOWER HERE...

"IT WAS EXCITING! I'M HAPPY I GAVE IT A SHOT!"

GUYS, IF WE KEEP THIS UP, IT'S GOING TO BE A FANTASTIC MUSICAL!

33

CHAPTER THREE

40

41

NO, **HE** WAS SUPPOSED TO SING WITH SHARPAY AND **I** WAS SUPPOSED TO WORK ON THE CHOREOGRAPHY WITH RYAN.

AND THE **NEXT** DAY?

NOTHING... JUST MORE PRACTICE, TESTS, PRACTICE, TESTS...

IF WE WERE **TRYING** TO AVOID EACH OTHER, WE'D HAVE A HARD TIME DOING IT BETTER THAN WE ARE NOW!

EAST HIGH, CHEMISTRY CLASS, ONE WEEK LATER.

DON'T TALK THAT WAY. YOU'RE GABRIELLA AND TROY, THE COOLEST COUPLE AT EAST HIGH!

YEAH, EVERYBODY SEEMS TO THINK SO, BUT...

...BUT WHAT IF WE **WEREN'T** ANYMORE?

DON'T YOU THINK YOU'RE GOING SLIGHTLY OVERBOARD?

MAYBE... MAYBE **NOT**. THIS MUSICAL IS TAKING UP SO MUCH OF OUR TIME THAT THERE'S NONE LEFT FOR US.

"TAKE YESTERDAY, FOR EXAMPLE..."

"OR THE DAY BEFORE..."

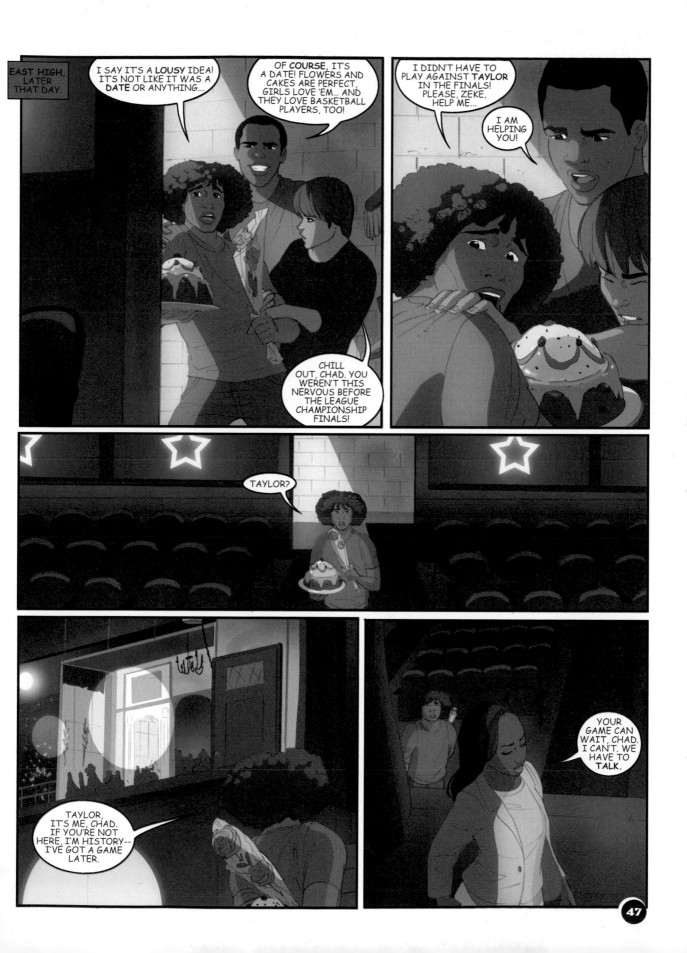

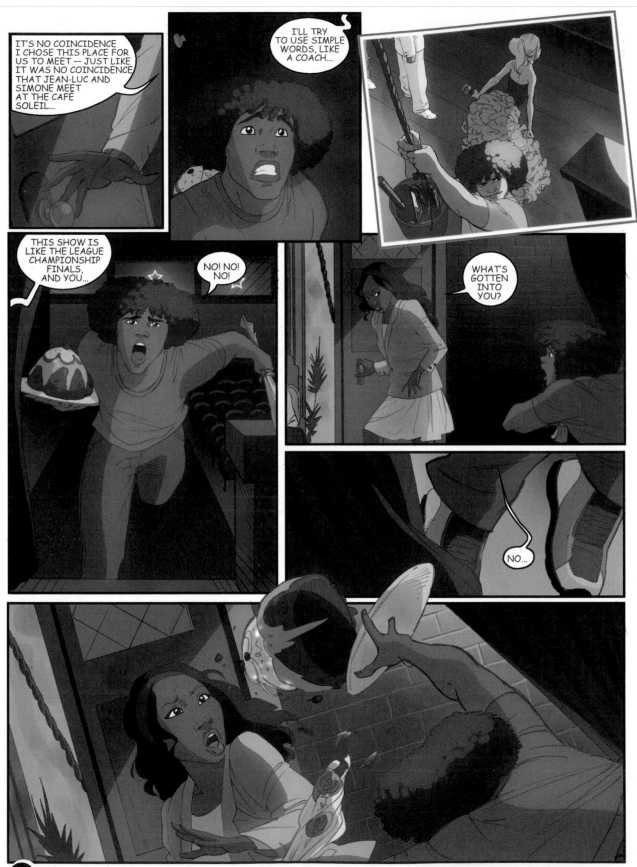

CHAPTER FOUR

CHAPTER FIVE

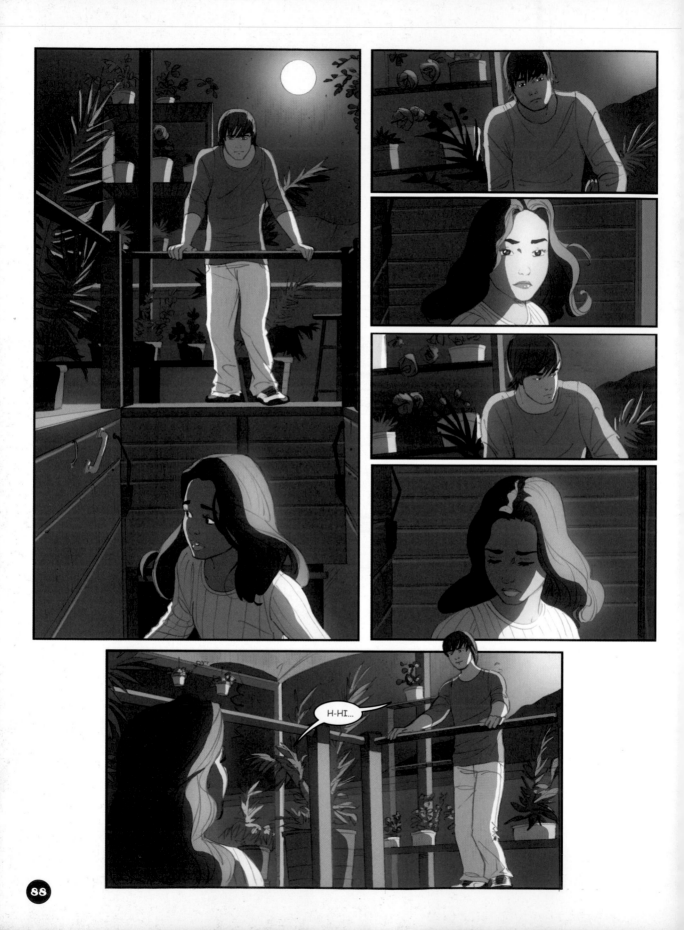

CHAPTER SIX